Intro

'Well, if you're happy to share your house with a ghost, that's ... ...,' said Lord Canterville. *'But please remember that I warned you.'*

When the American Ambassador, Hiram B. Otis, buys Canterville Chase from Lord Canterville, people try to warn him of the dangers. Everyone knows that the large old house is haunted by the famous Canterville Ghost – the ghost of Sir Simon de Canterville, who murdered his wife.

But Mr Otis and his wife and children are not worried about sharing their new home with a ghost. They are Americans and too modern to believe in ghosts. But they *do* see the ghost and, in their American way, they find him quite amusing – even when they clean a mysterious bloodstain from the library floor every day and it appears again the next morning!

The ghost becomes more and more unhappy. It is his duty to haunt the house, but the Americans aren't frightened by him, and the young Otis boys play terrible tricks on him. What can he do? How can he handle these annoying Americans?

The Canterville Ghost is one of three stories in this book. In the second story, *Lord Arthur Savile's Crime*, Lord Arthur meets the rather unpleasant Mr Podgers at one of Lady Windermere's parties, and his whole life changes. He had plans to marry Sybil Merton, one of the most beautiful girls in London. But now, before he can marry the lovely Sybil, he has to murder someone!

The third story, *The Sphinx Without a Secret*, is about the secret life of beautiful, mysterious Lady Alroy. It is also about the effect her unusual habits have on Lord Gerald Murchison, the man who wants to marry her. Lady Alroy lives in a house in the most expensive part of London, so why does she also rent a room in a building in one of the poorer streets? What does she do there? Who does she meet?

The writer of these stories, Oscar Wilde, was very successful in late Victorian London because of his short stories, plays and poems, but he was even more famous as one of the greatest characters of his day. He was born in Dublin, Ireland, on 16 October 1854 to Sir William Wilde and his wife Jane Francesca Elgee. Jane was a successful writer (she used the name 'Speranza' for her writing) and translator, and a strong supporter of an independent Ireland. She was also one of Dublin's most popular hostesses. Her fashionable Saturday afternoon meetings for writers and artists in the comfortable Wilde home were very enjoyable and full of exciting, intelligent conversation.

Oscar's father, Sir William, was Ireland's leading ear and eye doctor; he also wrote books about the country's early history and its traditional stories. In addition, in 1844 he gave the money to build a free eye hospital for Dublin's poor people. With this background, it is easy to understand how Oscar Wilde became a great writer, and even more admired for his conversation.

Young Oscar attended Portora Royal School from 1864 to 1871 and enjoyed summer holidays with his family in the country. He then studied at Trinity College, Dublin (1872–1874). He was an excellent student and continued his studies at Magdalen College, Oxford (1874–1878). While there he won a top prize for his poem *Ravenna*.

During his time at Oxford, he met other young men who believed that they could turn their lives into works of art. Oscar wore his hair long, dressed in unusual clothes and decorated his room with flowers and interesting pieces of art. He also became interested in nineteenth-century attitudes towards less traditional types of romantic love.

After his four years at Oxford, Wilde returned to Dublin and met and fell in love with Florence Balcome, but she loved Bram Stoker, the man who wrote *Dracula*. This caused Wilde to leave Dublin for London in 1878; he returned to Ireland for short visits only twice during the rest of his life.

In London, Wilde became more and more famous for his attitude to life and art and for his lifestyle. Gilbert and Sullivan, very well-known writers for the theatre, used Wilde as the model for the main character in one of their musical plays, *Patience*, in 1881.

As he became more famous, more opportunities came to Wilde. He was invited to New York at the end of 1881 and stayed in the United States for almost a year. He gave more than 140 speeches about his ideas on life and art and met many of the famous American writers of the day, including Henry Longfellow and Walt Whitman. His time in America gave him a clear picture of modern Americans, which he used in *The Canterville Ghost*.

When he returned to London, Wilde met and married Constance Lloyd, the daughter of a rich lawyer who had died when she was sixteen. Like Oscar's mother, Constance had a quick, independent mind and spoke several European languages. Constance's money gave the young couple quite a comfortable life. But they had two sons very quickly: Cyril was born in 1885 and Vyvyan in 1886. Their father needed to find ways to make more money.

Wilde took a job with a magazine (*The Woman's World*) in 1887 and began a very productive time. He wrote short stories, plays, poems and several books for children, including *The Happy Prince and Other Tales* for his sons in 1888. His most famous full-length book, *The Picture of Dorian Gray*, appeared in 1890. This is the strange and clever story of a man who does not show his age. He stays young and handsome for many years. At the same time, a picture of the man is hidden from the public. The man in the picture grows old and ugly as the years pass. The idea for the story came from Wilde's interest in art and beauty. It shows that strange things happen when someone loves beauty and the pleasures of life too much. This book is still popular today and has been used for a film and for several television programmes, but people in Victorian England were shocked by its dark, unusual subjects. People criticised the book because its ideas did not match society's ordinary ideas of good and bad. But Wilde replied with a simple statement: 'Books are well written or badly written.'

His first play, *Lady Windermere's Fan*, was performed in February 1892. Wilde surprised and amused the public on the first night with his unusual sense of fashion; he liked, for example, to wear a large green flower in his jacket. The play was a great success, and Wilde became the most popular British writer for the theatre at that time. *Lady Windermere's Fan* was followed by *A Woman of No Importance* (1893), *An Ideal Husband* (1895), and his greatest play, *The Importance of Being Earnest* (1895). This play looks at life in an unusual way. Unimportant things are very serious and important things are laughed at.

The plays were popular at the end of the nineteenth century and they are still popular today because Wilde had a great gift for writing clever and amusing conversation. They were successful because, as George Bernard Shaw said, 'He plays with everything.' In other words, Wilde changed people's way of looking at themselves and their society. The plays were imaginative, romantic, serious, emotional and, above all, very amusing. They had everything that Victorian theatre-goers were looking for, and the first night of a new Wilde play was a very exciting event.

Although he loved his wife, Wilde spent much of his life away from Constance and his sons. He had many rich and famous friends and was very close to one special man: Lord Alfred Douglas. The two men lived together and followed a way of life that was not accepted as normal in Victorian England. Douglas's father, an important member of the British upper-classes, was not happy about Wilde's interest in his son. He and Wilde began a terrible fight in the law courts. Wilde's friends advised him to leave England, but he stayed; he wanted to explain and to change people's thinking. But he lost and went to prison for two years. During this time Constance took the children to Switzerland and changed their surname from Wilde to Holland. Constance died in 1898.

Life in prison was very difficult, and Wilde's health suffered. He left prison on 19 May 1897 and decided to use the name Sebastian Melmoth. Oscar and Lord Alfred Douglas saw each other for a short time, but the relationship did not last. Wilde lived quietly and spent the last three years of his life away from society and the art world. With very little money, he had to stay with friends or live in cheap hotels in Paris. He wrote very little, but he produced the poem *The Ballad of Reading Gaol* (1898) to explain the terrible things he had experienced in prison.

Oscar Wilde died on 30 November 1900. Today many people still visit his last resting place in Paris.

Even more than a hundred years after his death, Oscar Wilde continues to be an important figure in modern society. Many books have been written about his life and works, and many films, television programmes, songs and amusing sayings have grown out of his ideas and writings. Oscar Wilde is remembered because his life was a work of art. People were shocked by his hair, his clothes, his flowers, and especially by his romantic ideas, but they were also greatly entertained. We remember Wilde's clever conversation and the characters in his plays because the plays are funny but they also carry a serious message. They show us how to look at life from new and different points of view. They are clever, amusing and very human, and we remember Oscar Wilde with love and admiration today.

The Canterville Ghost

When Hiram B. Otis, the American Ambassador, bought Canterville Chase, people told him that he was doing a very dangerous thing. There was no doubt that the place was haunted, they said. Lord Canterville himself told Mr Otis this when they were discussing the sale.

'We don't live in the place ourselves,' said Lord Canterville. 'Too many members of my family have seen the ghost. My aunt was dressing for dinner one night when she felt two skeleton's hands on her shoulders. The experience made her very ill, and she's never really got better again. After that, none of the younger servants wanted to stay with us, and my wife couldn't sleep there because of the noises at night.'

'Lord Canterville,' answered the Ambassador, 'I will buy the house, the furniture *and* the ghost. I come from a modern country where we have everything that money can buy. And if there *are* ghosts in Europe, I'll be happy to have one. I'll send it home to America, and people will pay to see it and to be frightened by it!'

Lord Canterville smiled. 'I'm afraid there really is a ghost,' he said. 'It's been famous for three centuries – since 1584. It always appears before the death of a member of our family.'

'Well, the family doctor appears too, I expect, Lord Canterville,' said the Ambassador. 'But the doctor is real, unlike the ghost. Believe me, there are no ghosts in any country in the world – not even in very old British families like yours.'

'Well, if you're happy to share your house with a ghost, that's all right,' said Lord Canterville. 'But please remember that I warned you.'

◆

1

A few weeks after this, the sale was completed and the Ambassador and his family went down to Canterville Chase by train.

Mrs Otis, when she was Miss Lucretia R. Tappen of West 53rd Street, had been a well-known New York beauty. She was now a fine-looking middle-aged woman, and in many ways she looked like an English lady. She was an excellent example of the fact that there is very little difference between the English and the Americans today, except, of course, for the language.

Her oldest son, Washington, was a fair-haired, rather good-looking young man. He was famous, even in London, as an excellent dancer. He was very sensible, except about certain flowers and about the important families of Europe.

Miss Virginia E. Otis was a lovely girl of fifteen, with large blue eyes. She was a good sportswoman, and loved to ride horses – and she could ride them faster than a lot of men. She had once raced old Lord Blinton on her horse twice round the park, winning easily. She looked wonderful that day, and when the young Duke of Cheshire saw her on horseback he immediately asked her to marry him! Sadly for him, his family sent him back to school that same night. He cried all the way there.

After Virginia came the twins. These were two happy little boys who laughed and shouted a lot. They liked to play tricks on people and were often punished for them.

Canterville Chase is seven miles from Ascot, the nearest railway station, so Mr Otis had arranged a carriage. He and his family started their drive very happily. It was a lovely July evening; birds were singing sweetly, and the fields and trees looked beautiful.

At the beginning of the journey, the sun was shining and the sky was blue. But when they reached Canterville Chase, storm clouds suddenly appeared in the sky. Before they reached the house, rain was falling heavily.

An old woman in a black dress was on the steps to greet them. She was Mrs Umney, the woman who looked after the house. Lady Canterville had asked Mrs Otis to continue Mrs Umney's employment as housekeeper at Canterville Chase, and Mrs Otis had agreed.

'Welcome to Canterville Chase,' Mrs Umney said to the Ambassador and his family.

She led them through the large hall into the library. This was a long low room, with a coloured window at one end. Tea was ready for them, so they took off their coats, sat down and began to look round the room. Mrs Umney poured the tea.

Suddenly, Mrs Otis noticed a dark red stain on the floor, near the fireplace.

'Something has made a stain there,' she said to Mrs Umney.

'Yes, madam,' replied the housekeeper in a low voice. 'It's a bloodstain.'

'How nasty!' cried Mrs Otis. 'I don't like bloodstains in a sitting room. It must go.'

The old woman smiled, and answered in the same low, mysterious voice. 'It's the blood of Lady Eleanore de Canterville,' she said.

'What happened to her?' asked Mrs Otis.

'She was murdered on that exact spot by her own husband, Sir Simon de Canterville, in 1575,' said Mrs Umney. 'Sir Simon lived for nine years after that, and then disappeared suddenly and very mysteriously. His body was never discovered, but his ghost still haunts the Chase. The bloodstain has always been admired by visitors to the house, and it can't be cleaned. People have tried, but it won't go away.'

'Of course it will!' cried Washington Otis. 'Pinkerton's Wonder Stain Cleaner will clean it in a second.'

And before the frightened housekeeper could stop him, he went down on his knees and began cleaning the floor with a small black stick. In a few minutes the bloodstain had disappeared.

'I knew Pinkerton could do it,' said Washington, and he looked round at his admiring family. But at that moment, lightning lit up the room and a terrible crash of thunder made them all jump up.

Mrs Umney fainted.

'What an awful climate!' said the American Ambassador calmly, as he lit a cigarette.

'Awful,' agreed his wife.

'This country is very full of people. I suppose they don't have enough good weather for everybody,' said Mr Otis.

Mrs Umney lay on the floor with her eyes closed. Mrs Otis looked down at her.

'My dear Hiram,' she cried, 'what can we do with a woman who faints?'

'Make her pay,' answered the Ambassador. 'She has to pay if she breaks something, so tell her to pay if she faints. She won't faint after that.'

And in a few moments Mrs Umney sat up. There was no doubt that she was very upset.

'Be careful,' she warned Mr Otis, and her voice was shaking. 'Trouble is coming to this house.'

'Trouble?' said Mr Otis. He smiled.

'I've seen things with my own eyes, sir, that would make your hair stand on end!' Mrs Umney continued. 'For many nights now I haven't closed my eyes in sleep. I've been too afraid.'

But Mr Otis and his wife told the woman not to worry.

'We're not afraid of ghosts,' said the Ambassador.

So the old housekeeper asked God to be kind to her new employers, made arrangements for an increase in her pay, and then went nervously up to her own room.

◆

The storm blew all night, but nothing mysterious happened. But the next morning, when the Otis family came down to breakfast, they found the terrible bloodstain on the library floor again.

'I don't think it can be the fault of Pinkerton's Wonder Stain Cleaner,' said Washington. 'I've used it for everything. It must be the ghost.'

He cleaned away the stain a second time with the little black stick, but the next morning it appeared again.

That night, Mr Otis closed all the windows, locked the library door, and carried the key upstairs. But in the morning the bloodstain was there again.

The whole family was very interested.

'Are there ghosts in the world, or aren't there?' they asked each other. They could not decide.

But that night, all doubts about the ghost left them for ever.

The day had been warm and sunny, and in the cool of the evening the family went out for a drive in the carriage. They did not return home until nine o'clock, when they had a light supper.

Their conversation did not include talk of ghosts or haunted houses, and no word was said about the dead Sir Simon de Canterville. Instead they spoke of happier things – the theatre, the actress Sarah Bernhardt, railway travel, Boston, New York, and many of the places that they had visited in America.

At eleven o'clock, they went to bed. By half-past eleven, all the lights in the house were out.

Some time later, Mr Otis was woken by a strange noise in the passage outside his room. It was the sound of metal rubbing against metal, and it seemed to come nearer to his bedroom door each minute. He lit a candle and looked at the clock on the small table next to his bed. It was exactly one o'clock.

Mr Otis was quite calm. He put a hand to his face and decided that he did not have a fever. Everything about him was quite normal.

His listened carefully for a few moments – and heard the sound of footsteps. He immediately got out of bed, took a small bottle out of his case, and opened the bedroom door.

He saw a terrible old man facing him in the pale moonlight. The old man's eyes were as red as fire, and he had long grey hair which fell over his shoulders. His clothes were in the style of an earlier century, and they were dirty and full of holes. Heavy, rusty chains hung from his arms and legs.

'My dear sir,' said Mr Otis, 'you really must put some oil on those rusty chains. For that purpose I'm giving you a small bottle of Smith's Rising Sun Oil. According to the makers, you only have to use it once. It's quite famous in America. Everybody uses it, and you will see that there are letters from well-known Americans printed on the bottle.'

Mr Otis put the bottle down on a small table.

'I'll leave it here for you,' he said. 'I'll be happy to give you more if you need it.'

Then the Ambassador went back to his bed.

For a moment, the Canterville Ghost did not move. He was shocked and angry. Then he knocked the bottle of oil violently on to the floor and hurried away down the passage. A strange green light shone out from his body, and he screamed – a deep and terrible cry – into the night.

When he reached the top of the great stairs, a door opened. Two little figures in white appeared out of the darkness, and a large pillow flew past his head! The ghost quickly did the only thing that seemed safe. He disappeared into the wall.

When he reached his secret room in the western part of the house, the ghost sat down in the moonlight and tried to think. He could not believe what had just happened. He had never been so insulted in all his 300 years of excellent and famous haunting!

To make himself feel better, he remembered some of his finest performances.

'There was Lord Canterville's aunt,' he said to himself. 'I put my skeleton hands on her shoulders and almost frightened her to death! That was wonderful! And before that there were the four girl servants. They ran away screaming after they saw me smiling at them through the curtains of the small bedroom! And there was the man-servant. He shot himself after he saw a green hand knocking at the window. Then there was the beautiful Lady Stutfield. She had to wear a black cloth round her neck to hide the mark of five skeleton fingers burnt into her white skin.'

The Canterville Ghost smiled to himself, but his smile quickly disappeared.

'And now? Now some terrible modern Americans come and offer me Rising Sun Oil, and throw pillows at my head! Well, I'll make them sorry! Oh, yes, I will!'

For the rest of that night, the ghost sat there, thinking deeply.

◆

The next morning, when the Otis family met at breakfast, they discussed the ghost for some time. The Ambassador was a little annoyed that his present had not been accepted.

'I don't wish to harm the ghost in any way,' he said. He looked at his young sons. 'And it is not polite to throw pillows at someone who has been in this house for so long.'

This was a very fair thing to say, but the twins shouted with laughter until Mr Otis looked coldly at them.

The Ambassador continued. 'But if the ghost refuses to use the Rising Sun Oil, we'll have to take his chains away from him. It's quite impossible to sleep with that noise outside the bedrooms every night.'

But for the rest of the week, the house was quiet. The only worrying thing was the bloodstain on the library floor. Each day Washington cleaned the floor with Pinkerton's Wonder Stain Cleaner, and each night Mr Otis locked the doors and windows.

But every morning the bloodstain was back again.

And, even stranger, it changed colour! Some mornings it was a dull red, then it was bright red, then a rich purple, and once a bright green. These changes amused the family, and every evening they tried to guess what colour it would be the next day.

Only little Virginia didn't seem to share the joke. For some reason she was upset at the sight of the bloodstain, and she very nearly cried on the morning when it was bright green.

The second appearance of the ghost was on Sunday night. Not long after they had gone to bed, the family were suddenly frightened by a terrible crash in the hall. Rushing downstairs, they found that a large suit of old armour had fallen from its usual place on to the stone floor. The Canterville Ghost was sitting in a sixteenth-century chair. He was rubbing his knees, with a look of great pain on his face.

The twins had brought their pea-shooters with them and immediately began to shoot dried peas at him, while Mr Otis aimed his gun.

'Hold up your hands!' said the Ambassador.

The ghost jumped up with a wild and angry cry and flew straight through them like the wind. He put out Washington's candle as he passed, and suddenly they were left in complete darkness.

When the ghost reached the top of the stairs, he turned and gave his terrible ghostly laugh. This famous laugh had been very useful on more than one occasion, turning Lord Raker's hair white, and causing three servants to run away in terror.

But before the sound died away, a bedroom door opened and Mrs Otis came out. She was carrying a bottle in her hand.

'I'm afraid you're not well,' she said to the Canterville Ghost. 'So I've brought you a bottle of Dr Dobell's Medicine. If you have stomach trouble, you will find that it's an excellent cure.'

The ghost stared angrily at her, and immediately began to make preparations to change himself into a large black dog. He

The twins had brought their pea-shooters with them . . .

was quite famous for this. But the sound of young footsteps coming up the stairs made him change his mind, and he disappeared with the deep cry of a dead man as the twins came near.

When he reached his room, the ghost became really unhappy. The twins' tricks were annoying, of course, but he was especially angry that he had not been able to wear the suit of armour. He hoped that even modern Americans would be excited at the sight of a Ghost in Armour.

It was his own suit. He had worn it with great success at Kenilworth in 1575, and Queen Elizabeth herself had said how handsome he looked. But when he had put it on for the Americans, the weight of the whole suit had been too great for him. He had fallen, hurting both his knees badly.

For some days after this, he was very ill. He only left his room to keep the bloodstain in good condition. But he took great care of himself, and he soon felt better. Then he decided to try, once again, to frighten the American Ambassador and his family.

He chose Friday, 17th August, for his appearance, and spent most of that day planning and preparing. He was going to wear a large hat, he decided, and the white burial sheet. And he would carry a rusty sword.

In the evening there was a violent storm. All the windows and doors in the old house shook noisily, and the rain crashed down on to the roof. It was perfect weather for haunting, and he loved it.

The ghost planned to start in Washington Otis's room. He was especially angry with that young man. He knew that Washington was the one who regularly used Pinkerton's Wonder Stain Cleaner to clean away the bloodstain. He intended to go quietly to Washington's room, make ghost noises at him, then cut his own throat to the sound of low music. This would fill the stupid young man with terror.

Next, he would go to the room of the Ambassador and

10

his wife. There he would place an ice-cold hand on Mrs Otis's face while he whispered the terrible secrets of death into her husband's ear.

He had not made a decision about little Virginia. She had never insulted him in any way, and she was pretty and gentle. Perhaps a few soft 'Aaaaghs!' from behind the curtains, he thought. Or if that did not wake her, a feverish movement of the blanket with ghostly fingers. He would decide later.

He was certainly going to frighten the twins, there was no doubt about that. Their beds were quite close to each other, so he would stand between them and appear like a green, icy-cold dead body until they were too frightened to move. Then he would throw off the white sheet and move round the room in his famous 'Skeleton's Dance', which had put terror into the hearts of many people.

At half-past ten, he heard the family going to bed. For some time he could hear shouts of laughter from the twins' room. Clearly they were amusing themselves with the light-hearted cheerfulness of schoolboys. But at a quarter past eleven everything was quiet, and at midnight the ghost left his room.

Night birds flew against the windows or screamed from trees. The wind blew round the outside of the house, and there were the usual ghostly midnight sounds, but the Otis family slept peacefully. They did not know about the terrible things that the Canterville Ghost had planned for them.

High above the noise of the rain and the storm, the Canterville Ghost could hear the heavy breathing of the Ambassador.

He stepped out of the wall with a cruel smile on his face, and the moon hid behind a cloud as he went past the great hall window. He moved in silence – a ghostly shadow. The darkness itself seemed to hate him as he passed through it. Once he thought he heard a shout, and he stopped. But it was only a dog from the farm near the house.

At last he reached the corner of the passage that led to the room of the unfortunate Washington. For a moment or two, the Canterville Ghost stopped and listened. The wind blew through his long grey hair. Then the clock sounded a quarter past midnight, and he laughed cruelly and turned the corner.

With a scream of terror, he stepped back and covered his face with his long, bony hands. There, facing him, stood a large ghostly figure with a shining, hairless head!

It was like something from a madman's dream! Silent, ugly laughter held open its great mouth. From inside it, a red light burned like a fire. The body was covered, like the Canterville Ghost's, in a burial sheet. There was a notice on it − a list, no doubt, of terrible things done in the past. The Canterville Ghost did not wait to read it. He had never seen a ghost before. It frightened him!

He gave it another quick look, then turned and ran. He fell over his own white sheet, dropped his rusty sword into one of Hiram B. Otis's shoes (where it was found the next morning), and ran back to his room. There he fell down on to his bed and hid his face under the blanket.

After a time, he began to feel better, and he decided to go and speak to the other ghost when daylight came.

'With the terrible twins,' he thought, 'two ghosts will be better than one!'

So, just as the early morning sun was touching the hills with silver light, he returned towards the place where he had first met the other ghost.

It was still there, but something had happened to it. The light had gone from its eyes, and it was resting against the wall like a sick man. The Canterville Ghost rushed forward and took it in his arms.

You can imagine his shock when the head fell off, and the body fell to pieces! He found himself holding a white curtain.

A sweeping brush and a round, hollow vegetable lay at his feet!

He couldn't understand it. He quickly took the piece of paper from the curtain and read:

> ## THE OTIS GHOST
> The only true and real ghost.
> All others are false.

Suddenly the Canterville Ghost understood. He had been tricked!

◆

The next day, the ghost was very weak and tired. The terrible excitement of the last four weeks was beginning to have its effect. For five days he stayed in his room, and at last he decided to stop putting the bloodstain on the library floor. If the Otis family did not want it, they clearly did not deserve it.

Ghostly appearances were a different thing and not under his control. It was his duty to appear in the passages once a week, and to make frightening noises from the great hall window on the first and third Wednesdays of every month. He had to do it. It is true that his life had been very bad, but he had a strong sense of duty in connection with his haunting work.

So, for the next three Saturdays, the Canterville Ghost walked the passages of Canterville Chase between the hours of midnight and three o'clock. He made sure that no-one heard or saw him. He took off his boots, walked as quietly as possible on the old floors of the house, wore a big black coat, and used the Rising Sun Oil on his chains. It is true that he only forced himself to use the oil with great difficulty. But one night, while the family were at dinner, he went into Mr Otis's bedroom and took the bottle.

Although he was very careful, he was not allowed to haunt without interruption. Strings were stretched across the passages,

The only true and real ghost.
All others are false.

THE OTIS GHOST

*Suddenly the Canterville Ghost understood.
He had been tricked!*

and he fell over them in the dark. And once he had a bad fall after stepping on some butter that the twins had put on the top of the stairs.

This last insult made him very angry, and he decided to visit the boys in his famous appearance as 'Rupert, the Headless Lord'.

He had not appeared as this for seventy years, not since he had frightened the pretty Lady Barbara Modish. It took him three hours to get ready, but at last he was very pleased with his appearance. The big leather riding boots that went with the clothes were just a little too large for him, and he could only find one of the two big guns, but he was quite satisfied. At a quarter past one he began his silent walk down the passage.

When he reached the twins' room, he saw that the door was not completely closed. The ghost pushed it open wide and walked in − and a heavy bucket of water fell from the top of the door, wetting him to the skin, and just missing his left shoulder! At the same time he heard shouts of laughter from the twins.

The great shock made him run back to his room as fast as he could go, and the next day he was ill with a bad cold.

◆

The Canterville Ghost now gave up all hope of ever frightening this rude American family. He moved round the passages wearing soft shoes, but only when he was sure that he would not meet anybody.

The last terrible experience was on 19th September. He went down to the entrance hall. The time was about a quarter past two in the morning, and he felt sure that he would be safe there. He was going towards the library to see if any of the bloodstain was left when suddenly two figures jumped out at him from a dark corner. They waved their arms wildly above their heads, and screamed out 'BOO!' in his ear.

The ghost was very frightened and rushed towards the stairs.

But Washington Otis was waiting for him there with a big bottle of Gardener's Grass Grower, ready to pour over him. With enemies on every side, the ghost had to disappear into the great fireplace to escape. (Fortunately the fire was not lit.) From there, he had to reach his room through the chimneys, and when he arrived back he was terribly dirty and untidy.

◆

After that, nobody saw him again. The twins tried to catch him several times, but the tricks only annoyed their parents and the servants. It was soon clear that the ghost's feelings were very badly hurt and that he would not appear.

Mr Otis began work again, writing his book about American politics. Mrs Otis gave a number of parties of the American kind, and surprised everybody in that part of the country. The twins played in the house and gardens. And Virginia rode round the roads on her little horse with the young Duke of Cheshire, who had come to spend the last week of the school holidays at Canterville Chase.

Mr Otis wrote a letter to Lord Canterville, telling him that the ghost was gone. Lord Canterville replied, saying that he was happy to hear it.

But the ghost was still in the house. It is true that he felt very ill, but he was not ready to give up. When he heard that the young Duke of Cheshire was in the Chase, he made arrangements. He planned to make his most frightening appearance as the 'Ghost of the Moonlit Murderer'. He remembered how it had frightened old Lady Startup on New Year's Day in 1764. She had screamed and fainted, and had died three days later.

But at the last moment, his terror of the twins stopped the ghost leaving his room, and the little Duke of Cheshire slept in peace and dreamed of Virginia.

A few days after this, Virginia and her young admirer went out riding in the fields. But a tree tore her riding skirt very badly, and when they got home she went up the back stairs to mend it. She was running past the half-open door of one of the rooms when she saw someone inside. It was, she thought, her mother's servant, who sometimes took her needlework there. So she went to the door to ask the girl to mend her skirt.

But to her great surprise, it was the Canterville Ghost himself! He was sitting by the window, watching the first leaves of autumn falling from the trees. His head was on his hand, and he looked terribly unhappy. Little Virginia's first idea was to run away and lock herself in her room, but then she began to feel sorry for him.

He didn't know she was there until she spoke to him.

'I'm so sorry for you,' she said. 'But my brothers are going back to school tomorrow, and then, if you behave yourself, no-one will annoy you.'

The ghost looked round in surprise at the pretty little girl who was daring to speak to him. 'It's silly to ask me to behave myself,' he answered. 'Very silly.'

'Why?' she said.

'Because I have to make noises with my chains, and cry through keyholes, and walk about at night,' said the Canterville Ghost. 'It's my only reason for being alive.'

'That's no reason for being alive, and you know you've been very bad,' said Virginia.

The ghost said nothing.

'Mrs Umney told us, when we arrived here, that you killed your wife,' Virginia continued.

'Well, yes, that's true,' said the ghost, sounding rather annoyed.

His head was on his hand, and he looked terribly unhappy.

'But it was a family matter, and nobody else's business.'

'It's very wrong to kill someone,' said Virginia.

'Oh, it's easy for people to blame me when they don't understand!' replied the Canterville Ghost. 'My wife was plain – even ugly – and she was a bad housekeeper. She knew nothing about cooking. But it doesn't matter now; it was a long time ago. But I don't think it was very nice of her brothers to make me die of hunger, even if I did kill her.'

'Die of hunger?' said Virginia. 'Oh, Mr Ghost – I mean Sir Simon – are you hungry? I have a sandwich in my case. Would you like it?'

'No, thank you,' said the ghost. 'I never eat anything now. But it's very kind of you. You're much nicer than the rest of your nasty, rude, dishonest family.'

'Stop!' cried Virginia angrily. 'You're the one who's rude and nasty. And if we're talking about dishonesty, you know you stole the paints out of my box to make that silly bloodstain in the library.'

The ghost was silent.

'First you took all my red colours, and I couldn't paint any more pictures of the sun going down in the evenings,' Virginia continued. 'Then you took the green and the yellow. In the end I only had dark blue and white, so I could only paint moonlight scenes, which are very difficult. I never told the others about it, although it was very annoying and silly. Who has ever heard of bright green blood?'

'Well, really,' said the ghost, rather ashamed, 'what could I do? It's very difficult to get real blood these days. And because your brother started the fight with his Wonder Stain Cleaner, it seemed all right to take your paints. What's wrong with that? You Americans don't understand anything.'

'You don't know anything about Americans or America,' said Virginia. 'Why don't you go there? Father will be happy to pay for your ticket to travel on a ship. There are people in America who would pay a hundred thousand dollars to have a family ghost.'

'No, thank you,' said the ghost. 'I don't think I'd like America.'

'Why? Because it doesn't have any terrible old houses?' said Virginia. 'Because everything's new and modern?' She was angry now. 'Excuse me. I'll go and ask my father to give the twins another week's holiday!'

'Please don't go, Miss Virginia,' cried the ghost. 'I'm so lonely and unhappy, and I really don't know what to do. I want to go to sleep, but I can't.'

'That's silly!' she said. 'You just go to bed and blow out the candle. There's no difficulty about sleeping. Even babies know how to do that, and they aren't very clever.'

'I haven't slept for 300 years,' the ghost said sadly.

Virginia's beautiful blue eyes got bigger and bigger with surprise. 'Three hundred years!' she said.

'Yes,' said the ghost. 'And I'm so tired.'

Virginia's little lips began to shake like the leaves of a flower, and she came towards him. She looked into his old, tired face.

'Poor, poor Ghost,' she said quietly. 'Isn't there a place where you can sleep?'

'Far away beyond the woods,' he answered in a low dreamy voice, 'there's a little garden by an old empty church. There the grass grows long and deep, and there are the white stars of wild flowers. A little bird sings all night, and the cold moon looks down, and the big old tree stretches out its arms over the sleepers.'

Virginia's eyes filled with tears, and she hid her face in her hands. 'You – you mean the Garden of Death,' she whispered.

'Yes, Death,' said the ghost. 'Death must be so beautiful. Lying in the soft brown earth, with the grass waving above your head, and listening to silence. I'd love to have no yesterday, and no tomorrow – to be at peace!' He looked at her. 'Have you ever read the old words on the library window?'

'Oh, often,' cried the little girl. 'I know them quite well. They're painted in old black letters that are hard to read. There are only four lines:

When a golden girl prays for you,
When a small child cries, too,
Then the whole house will be still
And peace will come to Canterville.

But I don't know what they mean.'

'They mean this,' the Canterville Ghost said sadly. 'You can cry for me, and for everything that I've done wrong, because I have no tears. You can pray with me, because I'm bad and can't pray. And then, if you've always been sweet and good and gentle, Death will be kind to me. You'll see terrible shapes in the darkness, and ghostly voices will whisper in your ear, but they won't harm you. They can't win the fight against the innocence and goodness of a child.'

Virginia did not answer, and the ghost looked down unhappily at her golden head.

Suddenly she stood up, very pale, and with a strange light in her eyes.

'I'm not afraid,' she said clearly. 'I'll pray for you to die, and for you to have peace.'

He stood up with a faint cry of happiness. Taking her hand, he bent over it and kissed it. His fingers were as cold as ice and his lips burned like fire, but Virginia went with him as he led her across the room.

At the end of the room, he stopped. He said some words that she could not understand. She saw the wall slowly open, and there was a great black hole in front of her. A bitter cold wind pulled at them, and in a moment the wall had closed behind them and the room was empty.

♦

About ten minutes later, the bell rang for tea, but Virginia did not come down from her room. Mrs Otis sent a servant to fetch her, but after a little time he came back.

'I can't find Miss Virginia anywhere,' he said.

At first, Mrs Otis did not worry. She knew that Virginia liked to go out into the garden in the evenings to get flowers for the dinner-table. But at six o'clock she sent the twins out to look for their sister while she and Mr Otis searched every room in the house.

At half-past six the boys came back.

'We can't find Virginia anywhere,' they said.

Everyone was now very anxious. They searched the house again, and then the gardens and the park. Next they searched the woods and fields round Canterville Chase, but they still could not find Virginia.

Mr Otis, Washington and two male servants went into the village.

'Have you seen Virginia?' they asked people.

But nobody could help.

When it was almost midnight, they went back to the house. They were very worried, but they could do nothing more until the morning.

Everyone was in the hall when the clock sounded midnight. Suddenly they heard a loud noise, followed by a terrible cry. A crash of thunder shook the house, and the sound of ghostly music filled their ears.

A secret door in the wall at the top of the stairs opened . . . and Virginia stepped out. She looked very pale, and there was a little jewel box in her hand.

They all rushed to her. Mrs Otis took her in her arms; the Duke of Cheshire could not stop kissing her; the twins went into a wild war dance round the group.

'Where have you been?' said Mr Otis. 'We looked everywhere for you! Your mother's been frightened to death. You must never play these tricks again!'

'Except on the ghost! Except on the ghost!' shouted the twins, laughing and dancing about.

'My dear little girl, thank God you're safe,' said Mrs Otis. 'You must never leave my side again, Virginia.' And she kissed the shaking child and put a hand in the golden hair.

'Father,' said Virginia quietly, 'I've been with the Ghost. He's dead, and you must come and see him. He was very bad, but he was also really sorry for everything that he did. He gave me this box of beautiful jewels before he died.'

They stared at her in surprise, but she led them through the opening in the wall and down a narrow secret passage. It was lit by a candle that Washington was holding in his hand. Finally they came to a great black door. Virginia touched it, and it moved back heavily. They stepped into a little low room with a stone ceiling and one very small window.

There was a large iron ring in the wall, and they saw a skeleton chained to it. The skeleton was lying on the stone floor. It seemed to be reaching for a wooden plate and a water pot which had been placed just too far away from it.

Virginia put her hands together and began to pray silently. The others looked down at the skeleton of Sir Simon de Canterville.

'God has forgiven him,' said Virginia, and a beautiful light seemed to appear around her face.

'What a wonderful person you are!' cried the young Duke of Cheshire, and he kissed her.

◆

Four days later, at about eleven o'clock at night, they put Sir Simon de Canterville into the ground under the old tree, in the Garden of Death, where he wanted to be. Lord Canterville came especially from Wales to be there with the Otis family.

Virginia put white flowers on the ground and, as she did this, the moon came out from behind a cloud and filled the Garden of Death with a silver light. At the same time, a little night bird began to sing.

The next morning, before Lord Canterville left, he and Mr Otis talked about the jewels, which were quite beautiful and very valuable.

'Lord Canterville,' said Mr Otis, 'these jewels belong to your family. I must ask you to take them to London with you. Virginia asks for only one thing – the box in which they were kept. Can she have it?'

'My dear sir,' said Lord Canterville, 'your lovely little daughter has been a good friend to one of my family – Sir Simon – and we'll always be grateful to her for that. She was wonderfully brave. Now, you remember that you bought the furniture *and* the ghost. The ghost's jewels are now yours. They are clearly your daughter's, and she must keep them. When she's a woman, she'll be pleased to have pretty things to wear. And if I dared to try and take the jewels, awful old Sir Simon would probably be back very quickly, giving me a terrible time!'

So Virginia kept the jewels, and she wore them in the spring of 1890 when she married the young Duke of Cheshire.

Some time after they were married, they went to Canterville Chase. On the day after they arrived, they walked to the old church. The Duchess had brought some lovely roses, and she put them under the old tree.

The Duke took her hands, and stood looking into her beautiful eyes.

'Virginia,' he said, 'a wife should have no secrets from her husband.'

'Dear Cecil!' said Virginia. 'I have no secrets from you.'

'Yes, you have,' he answered, smiling. 'You never told me what happened to you when you were locked up with the ghost.'

'Please don't ask me, Cecil,' she said. 'I can't tell you. Poor Sir Simon! I have so much to thank him for. Yes, don't laugh, Cecil. I really do. He made me see what Life is, and what Death means, and why Love is stronger than both.'

The Duke kissed his wife lovingly.

'You can have your secret if I can have your heart,' he whispered.

'You have always had that, Cecil,' she said.

'And you will tell our children one day?' he said.

Virginia did not answer, but her face went prettily red.

Lord Arthur Savile's Crime

A Study of Duty

It was Lady Windermere's last party of the season, and her London house was even more crowded than usual. Six government ministers were there, and all the women wore their prettiest dresses. At the end of a long room, with Lady Windermere's finest pictures on the walls around her, a German princess was talking bad French and laughing loudly at everything that was said to her. Some of the most intelligent people in London were discussing important matters in the supper room. It was one of Lady Windermere's best parties, and the princess stayed until nearly half past eleven.

Lady Windermere was forty years old, childless, and had that enjoyment of pleasure that is the secret of staying young. When the princess had gone, she went to talk to the Duchess of Paisley.

'Where's my chiromantist?' she asked the Duchess.

'Your what, Gladys?' said the Duchess.

'My chiromantist, Duchess,' said Lady Windermere. 'I can't live without him.'

The Duchess tried to remember what a chiromantist was, but she couldn't. She hoped it was not the person who looked after Lady Windermere's feet!

'He comes to see my hand twice a week, regularly,' continued Lady Windermere. 'He's very interesting about it.'

'Really!' the Duchess said to herself. 'He looks after feet, but he does hands too. How terrible!'

'I must introduce him to you,' said Lady Windermere.

'Introduce him!' cried the Duchess. 'You mean he is here?'

'Of course he's here. He always comes to my parties. My

hand, he tells me, shows that I can guess the future. And if my thumb was a little shorter, I'd be one of those people who are always very unhappy about the state of the world.'

'Oh, I understand now!' said the Duchess, feeling happier. 'He tells fortunes.'

'And misfortunes, too,' answered Lady Windermere. 'Plenty of them. For example, next year I'm in great danger on land and sea. It's all written down on my little finger, or on my hand – I forget which.'

'How exciting,' said the Duchess.

'Really, everyone should have their hands read once a month,' Lady Windermere continued. 'It doesn't change what's going to happen, but it's nice to be warned. Now, if someone doesn't go and fetch Mr Podgers at once, I'll have to go myself.'

'Let me go, Lady Windermere,' said a tall, handsome young man who was standing near them. He was listening to the conversation with an amused smile.

'Thank you, Lord Arthur,' said Lady Windermere. 'But I'm afraid you wouldn't recognize him.'

'If he's as wonderful as you say, Lady Windermere, I'm sure I'll know him,' said the young man. 'But tell me what he's like, and I'll bring him to you immediately.'

'Well, he isn't like a chiromantist,' said Lady Windermere. 'I mean he isn't mysterious or romantic-looking. He's a small fat man, without much hair on his head, and with big gold glasses. He looks like a family doctor. People are annoying in that way. My musicians look like writers of poems, and my writers look like musicians. Ah, here's Mr Podgers! Now, Mr Podgers, I want you to read the Duchess of Paisley's hand. Duchess, you must take your glove off. No, not the left hand – the other one.'

'Dear Gladys, I really don't think it's quite right,' said the Duchess.

'Nothing interesting is ever quite right,' said Lady Windermere.

'But I must introduce you. Duchess, this is Mr Podgers, my chiromantist. Mr Podgers, this is the Duchess of Paisley. If you say that she has more interesting hands than I have, I'll never believe in you again.'

'I'm sure, Gladys, that my hands are quite ordinary,' said the Duchess seriously.

'Let's see,' said Mr Podgers, looking at the little fat hand with its short square fingers. 'The line of life is excellent. You'll live to a great age, Duchess, and be very happy. The line of the heart–'

'Now please find something embarrassing, Mr Podgers,' cried Lady Windermere.

'It would give me great pleasure,' said Mr Podgers, 'if the Duchess were ever embarrassing. But I'm afraid I can only see a loyal person with a strong sense of duty.'

'Please continue, Mr Podgers,' said the Duchess. She seemed to be enjoying it now.

'Economy is one of your finest qualities,' continued Mr Podgers, and Lady Windermere began laughing loudly.

'Economy is a very good thing,' said the Duchess. 'When I married Paisley, he had eleven castles, and not one house that we could live in.'

'And now he has twelve houses and not one castle,' said Lady Windermere. 'You must read some more hands for us, Mr Podgers. You, Sir Thomas, show Mr Podgers yours.'

A cheerful-looking old gentleman came forward and held out a thick, strong hand with a very long third finger.

Mr Podgers looked at it. 'You're an adventurous person,' he said. 'There are four long voyages in your past, and one in the future. Three times you've been on ships that have gone down to the bottom of the sea. No, only twice, but you'll be in danger of it on your next journey. You're always on time for appointments, and you love collecting things. You had a serious illness between the ages of sixteen and eighteen. You hate cats.'

'How very clever!' said Sir Thomas. 'You must read my wife's hand, too.'

'Your second wife's,' said Mr Podgers quietly, still keeping Sir Thomas's hand in his. 'Your second wife's. I shall be glad to.'

But the lady did not want other people to know about her past or her future, and she was not the only one. A number of people seemed afraid to face the strange little man with his fixed smile, his gold eyeglasses, and his bright little green eyes.

But Lord Arthur Savile was watching Mr Podgers with a great amount of interest, and he was filled with the desire to have his own hand read. He was a little shy about asking the chiromantist, so he asked Lady Windermere. Did she think Mr Podgers would mind reading his hand?

'Of course he won't mind,' said Lady Windermere. 'That's what he's here for. All my guests do what I tell them to do. But I must warn you that I shall tell Sybil everything he says.'

'You will?' said Lord Arthur.

'Yes,' said Lady Windermere. 'She's coming to lunch with me tomorrow. If Mr Podgers discovers that you have a bad temper, or a wife hidden away somewhere, I'll certainly tell her about it.'

Lord Arthur smiled. 'I'm not afraid,' he said. 'Sybil knows me as well as I know her.'

'I'm a little sorry to hear you say that,' said Lady Windermere. 'A future wife ought not to know everything about the man she's going to marry.'

She turned to the small fat man.

'Mr Podgers, Lord Arthur Savile would like you to read his hand,' she said. 'Don't tell him that he's going to marry one of the most beautiful girls in London, because that was in the newspapers a month ago. But be sure to tell us something nice. Lord Arthur is one of my special favourites.'

'I'll try,' said Mr Podgers.

But when he saw Lord Arthur's hand, he became pale and said

*But when he saw Lord Arthur's hand, he became
pale and said nothing.*

nothing. His body seemed to shake, and his fat fingers grew cold.

Lord Arthur noticed these things, and for the first time in his life he felt afraid. He wanted to rush out of the room, but he controlled himself.

'I'm waiting, Mr Podgers,' he said.

'We're all waiting,' cried Lady Windermere impatiently. 'I believe Arthur is going on the stage, and you're afraid to tell him.'

But the chiromantist did not reply. Suddenly he dropped Lord Arthur's right hand and took his left. He bent down very low to examine it and his glasses almost touched it.

'What is it?' said Lady Windermere.

For a moment the chiromantist's face became white with shock and fear, but at last he said to Lady Windermere with a forced smile, 'It's the hand of a very nice young man.'

'Of course it is!' answered Lady Windermere. 'But will he be a good husband? That's what I want to know.'

'All nice young men are good husbands,' said Mr Podgers.

'Yes, yes!' said Lady Windermere. 'But I want details, Mr Podgers. Details are what matter. What's going to happen to Lord Arthur?'

'Well, Lord Arthur will go on a journey soon,' said Mr Podgers.

'Oh yes, after his marriage, of course!'

'And lose one of his relatives,' said Mr Podgers.

'Not his sister, I hope?' said Lady Windermere.

'Certainly not his sister,' answered Mr Podgers. 'Not a close relative.'

'Is that all?' said Lady Windermere. She did not look pleased. 'I won't have anything interesting to tell Sybil tomorrow. Nobody cares about relatives who aren't close these days – it's not fashionable. Now let's all go in and have supper.'

But Lord Arthur had a terrible feeling of fear – the fear of something very bad. He only just heard Lady Windermere's call to follow her and the others into the next room for supper. He thought about Sybil Merton, and his eyes began to fill with tears. Could something come between them? Suddenly, Mr Podgers came back into the room. When he saw Lord Arthur, the chiromantist stopped suddenly and his fat face went a greenish-yellow colour. The two men looked at each other, and for a moment there was silence.

'The Duchess has left one of her gloves here,' said Mr Podgers at last. 'She asked me to bring it to her. Oh, here it is.'

'Mr Podgers, I want you to give me an answer — a true answer — to the question that I am going to ask you,' said Lord Arthur.

'Another time, Lord Arthur,' said Mr Podgers. 'I must take the Duchess her glove.'

'Don't go,' said Lord Arthur. 'The Duchess is in no hurry.'

He walked across the room and held out his hand.

'Tell me what you saw there,' he said. 'I must know. I'm not a child.'

Mr Podgers' eyes looked unhappy behind his glasses, and he moved from one foot to the other.

'What makes you think that I saw anything else in your hand, Lord Arthur?' he asked the other man.

'I know you did. I demand that you tell me what it was,' said Lord Arthur. 'I'll pay you. I'll give you a hundred pounds.'

The chiromantist's green eyes became bright — but only for a moment.

'I'll send you a cheque tomorrow,' said Lord Arthur. 'Where shall I send it?'

'Let me give you my card,' said Mr Podgers. And he gave Lord Arthur a rather large card. On it was printed:

> ## MR SEPTIMUS R. PODGERS
> *Chiromantist*
> 103a West Moon Street, London

'Be quick,' cried Lord Arthur. His face was pale, but he held out his hand.

Mr Podgers looked nervously round. 'It will take a little time, Lord Arthur,' he said.

'Be quick, sir!' cried Lord Arthur again.

Mr Podgers took off his glasses, cleaned them, and put them back on again. Then he smiled.

'I'm ready now,' he said.

◆

Ten minutes later, Lord Arthur Savile rushed out of Lady Windermere's house. His face was white with terror and his eyes were wild with unhappiness.

The night was very cold, and a there was a sharp wind, but his hands were hot with fever and his face burned like fire. Once he stopped under one of the gas lamps in the square. He looked at his hands, and thought he could already see the stain of blood on them. A faint cry came from his shaking lips.

Murder! That is what the chiromantist saw there. Murder! And the night seemed to know it. The dark corners of the streets were full of murder. Murder laughed at him from the roofs of the houses.

'Murder! Murder!' he repeated, as he walked and walked through the city. The sound of his own voice made him shake. He felt a mad desire to stop a man who was passing and tell him everything.

At the corner of Rich Street, he saw two men reading a large notice on the wall. He went to look at it. As he came near, he saw the word 'MURDER' printed in black letters. It was a police advertisement offering a reward for information about a man between thirty and forty years of age, with a scar on the right side of his face.

Lord Arthur read it again and again. Would the man be

caught? How did he get the scar?

'Perhaps one day my name will appear on a notice like this,' he thought. 'Lord Arthur Savile – wanted for murder!'

The thought made him sick, and he hurried into the night.

He did not know where he went, and it was just before daylight when he found himself in Piccadilly. By the time he reached his home in Belgrave Square, the sky was a faint blue, and birds were beginning to sing in the gardens.

◆

When Lord Arthur woke, it was twelve o'clock. The midday sun was coming through the curtains of his room. He got up and looked out of the window. Some children were playing happily below him in the square, and the street was crowded with people on their way to the park.

He had a bath and some breakfast, then lit a cigarette and sat down to think. On the shelf, facing him, was a large photograph of Sybil Merton as he had seen her first. It had been at Lady Noel's party.

The small, perfectly shaped head was bending a little to one side. It seemed that the thin, pretty neck could only just carry the weight of so much beauty. The lips were not quite closed, and they seemed ready to make sweet music. All the innocence and sweetness of a young girl looked out from the dreamy eyes.

As Lord Arthur looked at the photograph, he was filled with the terrible pity that comes from love. How could he marry her now, when murder lay ahead? At any moment he might have to do the awful thing that was written in his hand. What happiness could there be for them with that in his future?

He must stop the marriage – that was clear to him. He loved Sybil with all his heart, but he knew what his duty was. He had no right to marry her until after the murder.

He must do the murder first – and soon. Many men would

prefer to do nothing. They would let time decide what happened. But Lord Arthur's sense of duty was too strong for that.

For a time, it is true, he felt badly about what he had to do. But these feelings did not continue. The wild terror of the night before was gone. He saw his duty clearly now, and he was going to do it.

There was only one question that troubled him. Who was going to be murdered? He knew that there must be a body in a murder, not just a murderer. Lord Arthur was not an especially clever person, so he had no enemies. And this was not the time, he felt, to satisfy his private dislike of someone.

So he made a list of his friends and relatives on a piece of paper, and after much thought he chose Lady Clementina Beauchamp from the list. He had always been very fond of Lady Clem, as everyone called her. She lived in Curzon Street and was his own second cousin – the daughter of his mother's cousin. This dear old lady's death could not possibly make him any richer. He already had plenty of money. She seemed to him to be just the right person. So, feeling that a delay would be unfair to Sybil, he decided to make his arrangements immediately.

First, of course, he had to write his cheque for the chiromantist. He sat down at the writing table near the window and did this. Then he put the cheque for a hundred pounds into an envelope and told a man-servant to take it to Podgers' address in West Moon Street. Next, he dressed to go out.

As he was leaving the room to go to his club, he looked back at Sybil Merton's photograph.

'She'll never know what I'm doing for her,' he told himself. 'I'll keep the secret hidden in my heart.'

On the way to the club, he stopped his carriage at a flower shop and sent Sybil a beautiful basket of spring flowers.

At the club, he went straight to the library, rang the bell, and ordered the waiter to bring him a drink and a book on poisons.

He had decided that poison was the best method. It was safe, sure and quiet, and it was not violent.

In Erskine's book on poisons, he found an interesting and complete description of the qualities and effects of aconitine, written in quite clear English. Aconitine seemed to be the poison he wanted. It worked quickly – it was almost immediate in its effect. It was perfectly painless when it was taken in the form of a capsule. He made a note of the amount that was necessary to cause death. Then he put the book back in its place on the shelf in the club library, and left.

He walked to Pestle and Humbey's, the famous London chemists. Mr Pestle himself came out to serve Lord Arthur. He was surprised at the order, and he asked about a doctor's note.

Lord Arthur explained that the poison was for a large dog that he had to destroy. 'The dog has already bitten one of the servants,' he said.

Mr Pestle was satisfied. He admired Lord Arthur's knowledge of poisons, and he had the capsule prepared immediately.

Lord Arthur put the capsule into a pretty silver box that he saw in a shop window in Bond Street. He threw away Pestle and Humbey's ugly little box, and went immediately to Lady Clementina's.

'Well, Arthur!' said the old lady, when he entered the room. 'Why haven't you been to see me recently, you bad boy?'

'My dear Lady Clem, I never have a free moment,' said Lord Arthur, smiling.

'I suppose you go about all day with that lovely Miss Sybil Merton, buying pretty things and making sweet lovers' talk,' said Lady Clementina.

'I promise you that I haven't seen Sybil for twenty-four hours, Lady Clem,' replied Lord Arthur.

'You haven't?' said Lady Clementina. 'Why not?'

'I think at the moment she belongs to her hat maker,' replied Lord Arthur.

'Of course,' said Lady Clementina. 'And that's the only reason you come to see an ugly old woman like myself. Here I am, a poor sick woman with a bad temper. Lady Jensen sends me all the worst French story-books she can find. Without them, I don't think I could get through the day. I see as many doctors as I can, but they can't even cure my stomach trouble.'

'I've brought you a cure for that, Lady Clem,' said Lord Arthur seriously.

'Have you?' said the old lady.

'Yes,' said Lord Arthur. 'It's a wonderful thing, invented by an American.'

'I don't think I like anything invented by Americans, Arthur,' said Lady Clementina. 'I read an American book the other day, and it was very silly.'

'Oh, but there's nothing silly about this, Lady Clem! It's the perfect cure. You must promise to try it.' And Lord Arthur took the little box out of his pocket and gave it to her.

'Well, the box is very pretty, Arthur,' she said. 'Is it really a present? That's very kind of you. And is this the wonderful medicine? It looks like a sweet. I'll take it immediately.'

'No, no, Lady Clem!' cried Lord Arthur. He caught hold of her hand. 'You mustn't do that. If you take it when you aren't in pain, it might do you a lot of harm. Wait until you have a stomach ache, and take it then. You'll be surprised at the result.'

'I'd like to take it now,' said Lady Clem, holding the little capsule up to the light. 'I'm sure it's nice. I hate doctors, but I love medicines. But I'll keep it until my next attack.'

'And when will that be?' Lord Arthur asked quickly. 'Will it be soon?'

'I hope not for a week,' she said. 'I had a very bad time yesterday morning.'

'But you will have one before the end of the month, Lady Clem?' asked Lord Arthur.

'I'm afraid so,' said Lady Clementina. She smiled at him. 'You're very kind to worry about me, Arthur, dear. But now you'll have to leave me. I have to go out to dinner with some very boring people. Goodbye. Give my love to Sybil. And thank you very much for the American medicine.'

'You won't forget to take it, Lady Clem, will you?' said Lord Arthur.

'Of course I won't, you silly boy,' she replied. 'You're really very kind. I'll write and tell you if I want any more.'

Lord Arthur left the house feeling very happy.

That night, he went to see Sybil Merton.

'Sybil,' he said. 'Because of a friend, I've been put in a very . . . difficult position. I have a duty to put this matter right, and until I do I'm not a free man. I'm afraid our marriage will have to wait.'

Sybil threw herself into his arms and began to cry.

'Please be patient, dear,' he said.

He stayed with her until nearly midnight. He told her that he loved her, and promised that everything would be all right in the end.

When he got home, he wrote a letter (full of words, but explaining little) to Sybil's father.

And early the next day, he left for Venice.

◆

In Venice Lord Arthur met his brother, Lord Surbiton, who had come from Corfu in his sailing boat. The two young men spent two very pleasant weeks together, but Lord Arthur was not completely happy. Every day he looked at the list of 'Deaths' in *The Times* newspaper, expecting to see a notice of Lady Clementina's death. But every day there was nothing. Had something happened to stop her taking the aconitine?

Sybil's letters made him sad, too. They were full of love, but she seemed to be unhappy. And sometimes he felt that he would never see her again.

After two weeks, Lord Surbiton got bored with Venice and the two brothers sailed down the coast to Ravenna. But after a time, Lord Arthur became anxious about Lady Clementina and he returned to Venice by train.

There were several messages for him at his hotel, and he opened them quickly. Everything had been successful! Lady Clementina had died quite suddenly five days ago!

His first thought was for Sybil, and he sent her a message – he was returning immediately to London. The other two messages for him were from his mother, the Duchess, and from Mr Mansfield, Lady Clementina's lawyer.

The old lady had gone to dinner with the Duchess on the night of her death. She had been very happy and full of fun, but had gone home rather early because of stomach trouble. In the morning she was found dead in her bed. The doctor said that her death was peaceful.

A few days before she died, Lady Clementina had made her will. In it she left her London house and all her furniture to Lord Arthur. The value of the property was not great, but Mr Mansfield wanted Lord Arthur to return immediately. There were a lot of bills to pay, he said.

Lord Arthur was deeply affected by Lady Clementina's kindness to him, and he blamed Mr Podgers – in a way – for her death. But his love of Sybil was stronger than any other feeling. He was glad that he had done the right thing.

The Mertons were happy to see him. Sybil made him promise that nothing would ever come between them again. The marriage was arranged for 7th June, and life seemed bright and beautiful again to Lord Arthur.

One day, he was in Lady Clementina's house with Mr Mansfield and Sybil. They were burning old papers and clearing things out of drawers. Suddenly Sybil gave a happy little cry.

'What have you found, Sybil?' said Lord Arthur, smiling.

'This little silver box, Arthur,' said Sybil. 'Isn't it beautiful? Please give it to me!'

It was the box that had held the aconitine.

Lord Arthur had almost forgotten about the box and the poison. Now, he remembered the terrible worry that he had suffered for Sybil. It seemed strange that she was the first person to remind him of it.

But he said, 'Of course you can have it, Sybil. I gave it to poor Lady Clem myself.'

'Oh, thank you, Arthur,' said Sybil. 'And please can I have the sweet too? I didn't know that Lady Clem liked sweets.'

Lord Arthur's face went pale, and when he spoke his voice was almost a whisper. 'Sweet, Sybil? What do you mean?' he said slowly.

'There's just one in the box,' she said. 'It looks quite old, and I don't really want to eat it. What's the matter, Arthur? You've gone very white!'

Lord Arthur rushed across the room and took the box. The capsule was there, with the aconitine liquid still in it. Lady Clementina had died a natural death!

The shock was terrible. He threw the capsule into the fire, and sat down and put his head in his hands.

◆

When Lord Arthur delayed the marriage for a second time, Mr Merton was quite upset. His wife had already ordered her dress for the wedding, and she tried to make Sybil take back her promise to marry Lord Arthur. But Sybil's love for the young man was too strong. Her mother could not say anything to change that.

Lord Arthur felt terrible for several days after his shock. But soon he realized what he had to do. Poison had failed. Next, he

. . . please can I have the sweet too?

would have to try a bomb. That seemed sensible.

He looked again at his list of friends and relatives. After careful thought, he decided to blow up his uncle, the Dean of Chichester.

The Dean was an important churchman. He also had a wonderful collection of clocks. It seemed to Lord Arthur that this interest in clocks gave him a perfect opportunity.

Where would he get a clock-bomb? This was, of course, a problem. Suddenly he thought of his friend Rouvaloff. Rouvaloff was a young Russian who strongly disliked the government of his country. He knew a lot about bombs and where to get them. Lord Arthur went to see the young man without delay.

'So you're taking a serious interest in politics?' said Rouvaloff, when Lord Arthur explained what he wanted.

Lord Arthur hated pretending. He had to say that he was not interested in politics. He wanted the bomb for a family matter.

Rouvaloff looked at him in surprise, but he saw that his friend was quite serious. He wrote an address on a piece of paper, and a letter introducing Lord Arthur, and gave them to him.

Lord Arthur thanked him, then took a carriage to Soho. There he walked until he came to a little street full of small houses. He knocked on the door of a little green house at one end.

After some minutes, the door was opened by a rough-looking German. 'What do you want?' he asked Lord Arthur.

Lord Arthur gave him the letter from Rouvaloff.

In England, the German was known as Winckelkopf. He read the letter and invited Lord Arthur into a very dark little room.

'I want to discuss some business with you,' said Lord Arthur. 'My name is Smith – Mr Robert Smith – and I want you to make me a clock-bomb.'

'I'm pleased to meet you, Lord Arthur,' said the cheerful little German, laughing.

'You know me?' said Lord Arthur.

'Yes, I know who you are,' said Winckelkopf. 'But please don't worry. It's my duty to know everybody, and I remember seeing you one evening at Lady Windermere's house. I hope she's well. Will you sit with me while I finish my breakfast? Let me get you a glass of wine.'

Lord Arthur was very surprised that he had been recognized. But he was soon sitting at the table, drinking a glass of very good German wine.

'Clock-bombs are not very useful when you are sending a bomb abroad,' said Winckelkopf. 'They usually explode before they reach their correct destination. But if you want to use one in this country, I can give you an excellent one. Can I ask who it is intended for? If it's for the police, I'm afraid I can't do anything for you. The English detectives are really our best friends. They're very stupid, and because of this we can do exactly what we like. I wouldn't want to kill even one of them.'

'It's not for the police,' answered Lord Arthur.

'Then who...?' began Winckelkopf.

'It's intended for the Dean of Chichester,' said Lord Arthur.

'Oh dear! I didn't know that you felt so strongly about religion, Lord Arthur,' said Winckelkopf. 'Not many young men do these days.'

'I'm afraid I don't deserve your high opinion, Winckelkopf,' said Lord Arthur. 'The fact is, I really know nothing about religion.'

'So it's a private matter?'

'Yes,' said Lord Arthur.

Winckelkopf left the room. He returned a few minutes later with a pretty little French clock. A small golden figure of Liberty stood on the top of it.

Lord Arthur smiled when he saw it. 'That's just what I want,' he cried. 'Now tell me how it works.'

'That's just what I want,' he cried. 'Now tell me how it works.'

'Ah! That's my secret,' answered Winckelkopf. 'Tell me when you want the explosion, and I'll arrange it. It will happen at exactly the right moment.'

'Well, today's Tuesday, and if you could send it to the Dean immediately . . .' began Lord Arthur.

'That's impossible,' said Winckelkopf. 'I have a lot of important work for some friends in Moscow. But I can send it tomorrow.'

'Oh, that will be soon enough,' said Lord Arthur. 'If it's delivered tomorrow night, or on Thursday morning, that will be fine. Friday, exactly at midday, would be perfect for the explosion. The Dean is always at home at midday on Fridays.'

'Friday at midday,' repeated Winckelkopf, and he made a note of the time.

'And now,' said Lord Arthur, standing up, 'how much should I pay you?'

'It's a very small matter, Lord Arthur,' said Winckelkopf. 'I can't really ask for anything. Shall we say five pounds? I'm happy to help a friend of Rouvaloff's.'

'But I must pay you for your time and trouble, Winckelkopf,' said Lord Arthur.

'Oh, that's nothing! It's a pleasure. I don't work for money. I live only for my art.'

Lord Arthur put five pounds on the table, thanked the German for his kindness, and left the house.

◆

Lord Arthur was almost too excited to sleep for the next two days. On Friday, at twelve o'clock midday, he went to his club to wait for news.

All afternoon, one of the club servants put up messages on the notice board, but they were all about horse races, parliament or the weather. At four o'clock, the evening newspapers arrived, and Lord Arthur took several of them into the library. He read them carefully, but there was nothing in them about the Dean of Chichester.

He went to see Winckelkopf the next day. The young German apologized many times, and offered to give him another clock-bomb. But Lord Arthur refused. He had decided that perhaps bombs were not the best idea.

Two days later, he was going upstairs at home when his mother, the Duchess, called out to him. Lord Arthur came back down and she showed him a letter from the Dean of Chichester's daughter.

'Jane writes very interesting letters,' the Duchess said. 'You really must read this one, Arthur.'

Lord Arthur read the letter quickly.

The Deanery, Chichester
27th May

My dearest Aunt,

We have had great fun with a clock that an unknown admirer sent to Father last Thursday. It arrived in a wooden box from London. Father thinks that it was sent by someone who has read his book, What is Liberty? On the top of the clock there was a small figure of Liberty.

Father put the clock above the fireplace in the library, and we were all sitting there on Friday morning when the clock sounded twelve. We heard a funny noise, then some smoke came from the bottom of the figure, and Liberty fell off! She broke her nose on the stone fireplace!

Maria was quite frightened, but it looked very funny. James and I laughed loudly, and even Father was amused. When we examined it, we found that it is an alarm clock. You put in some stuff to make a small explosion. Then it wakes you up with a loud noise at the hour you choose.

Father said it could not stay in the library because of the noise, so Reggie carried it away to the schoolroom. Now he makes small explosions there all day.

Reggie has just made another explosion, and Father has ordered the clock to be sent to the garden room. I don't think he likes it as much as he did at first, although he is pleased that someone sent it to him. It shows that people read his books and learn from them.

We all send our love and hope that Uncle Cecil's toe is better.

Your loving niece,

Jane Percy

Lord Arthur looked very serious and unhappy about the letter, and that made the Duchess laugh.

'My dear Arthur,' she cried, 'I'll never show you a young lady's letter again. But what can I say about the clock? I'd like to have one myself.'

'I don't like them,' said Lord Arthur, with a sad smile. He kissed his mother and left the room.

When he got upstairs, he threw himself into a chair, and his eyes filled with tears.

'I've done my best to complete this murder, but on both occasions I've failed,' he thought. 'And it hasn't been my fault! I've tried to do my duty!'

◆

At half past seven, Lord Arthur dressed and went to the club.

The doorman gave him a letter. It was from Winckelkopf, inviting him to come the next evening and look at an umbrella-bomb that had just arrived from Geneva. The umbrella exploded when you put it up.

Lord Arthur threw away the letter and went out. He walked down to the River Thames and sat for hours by the water. The moon looked down through an opening in the clouds. Sometimes a river boat went past him. The railway lights changed from green to red as trains went across the bridge. At twelve o'clock the big bell of the clock at Westminster sounded, and the night seemed to shake. Then the railway lights went out, and the noises of the city became quieter.

At two o'clock Lord Arthur stood up and walked slowly along beside the river. After some minutes, he saw a man looking over the riverside wall. As he came nearer, the man looked up, and the gaslight lit up his face.

It was Mr Podgers, the chiromantist! It was impossible to make a mistake about the fat, unhealthy face, the gold glasses, the weak smile, and the greedy mouth.

Lord Arthur stopped. A wonderful idea came into his mind, and he stepped quietly up behind Mr Podgers. Moving quickly, he picked up the chiromantist by the legs, and threw him over the wall into the river! There was a cry, the sound of a body hitting the water, and then silence.

Lord Arthur looked down, but there was no sign of Mr Podgers. Once he thought that he saw the fat little body swimming towards the steps at the bottom of the bridge. But when the moon came out from behind a cloud, there was nothing there.

'I've succeeded at last!' he thought. Then Sybil's name came to his lips.

'Have you dropped something, sir?' said a voice behind him suddenly.

He turned round and saw a policeman.

'Nothing important,' he answered, smiling.

◆

For the next few days Lord Arthur waited with feelings of hope, then of fear. There were moments when he almost expected Mr Podgers to walk into the room. Twice he went to the chiromantist's address in West Moon Street, but he was not brave enough to ring the bell.

Finally news came. He was sitting in the smoking-room of his club, having tea, when a waiter came in with the evening newspapers. A moment later Lord Arthur was turning the pages of one of them when he saw this:

DEATH OF A CHIROMANTIST
Yesterday morning, at seven o'clock, the body of Mr Septimus R. Podgers, the famous chiromantist, was washed on to the shore from the river at Greenwich, just in front of the Ship Hotel. The unfortunate gentleman disappeared a few days ago. It is believed that he killed himself after working too hard.

Lord Arthur rushed out of the club with the newspaper still in his hand. He went straight to the Mertons' house. Sybil saw him from a window, and she guessed from the look on his face that he brought good news. She ran down to meet him.

'Arthur, what– ?'

'My dear Sybil,' cried Lord Arthur, 'let's be married tomorrow!'

'You silly boy! We haven't ordered the wedding cake yet!' said Sybil, laughing through her tears.

◆

The wedding was three weeks later. The Dean of Chichester read the marriage service beautifully. Everybody agreed that they had never seen a happier-looking pair than Lord Arthur and Sybil.

Some years afterwards, Lady Windermere was on a visit to Lord and Lady Arthur Savile's lovely old home in the country. She and Sybil were sitting in the garden.

'Are you happy, Sybil?' asked Lady Windermere.

'Dear Lady Windermere, of course I'm happy!' said Sybil. 'Are you?'

'I have no time to be happy, Sybil,' said Lady Windermere. 'I always like the last person who is introduced to me. But when I know people, I get bored with them.'

'Are you still interested in chiromancy, Lady Windermere?' asked Sybil, looking at her guest's beautiful hands.

'Ah! You remember that nasty Mr Podgers, do you?' said Lady Windermere. 'He made me hate chiromancy. I'm interested in other things now.'

'You mustn't say anything against chiromancy here, Lady Windermere,' said Sybil. 'It's the only subject that Arthur doesn't like people to laugh about. He's quite serious about it.'

'You don't mean that he believes in it, Sybil?'

'Ask him, Lady Windermere,' said Sybil. 'Here he is.'

And Lord Arthur came up the garden with yellow roses in his hand, and their two children dancing round him.

'Lord Arthur,' said Lady Windermere.

'Yes, Lady Windermere,' said Lord Arthur.

'You don't believe in chiromancy, do you?'

'Of course I do,' said the young man, smiling.

'But why?' asked Lady Windermere.

'Because of chiromancy, I have all the happiness in my life,' he said, and sat down in a garden chair. He gave his wife the roses and looked into her lovely eyes. 'Because of chiromancy, I have Sybil.'

'How silly!' cried Lady Windermere. 'I've never heard anything so silly in all my life.'

The Sphinx Without a Secret

One afternoon I was sitting outside the Café de la Paix in Paris, watching the people passing along the street. I was wondering why some people were very poor while others were so rich.

Suddenly I heard somebody call my name.

I turned round and saw Lord Murchison. We had not met since we were at Oxford University together, nearly ten years before, and I was pleased to see him again. We shook hands warmly.

I had liked him very much at Oxford, and we had been very good friends. He had been so handsome, so full of life, and a very honest young man. We used to say that he would be the best person in the world if he was not always so honest. But I think we really admired him for his honesty.

Now, looking at him ten years later, he seemed different. He looked anxious and worried, and he seemed to have doubts about something. I could not believe that he was in doubt about religion or politics, because he always had such definite opinions about everything. So I thought the problem must be a woman.

I asked him if he was married yet.

'I don't understand women well enough to marry one,' he answered.

'My dear Gerald,' I said, 'it is our job to love women, not to understand them.'

'I can't love anyone that I can't trust,' he answered.

'I think you have a mystery in your life, Gerald,' I said. 'Tell me about it.'

'Let's go for a drive,' he answered. 'It's too crowded here. No, not a yellow carriage – there, that dark green one will be all right.'

And in a few moments we were driven away from the café.

'Where shall we go to?' I said.

'Oh, I don't mind!' he answered. 'The restaurant in the Bois de Boulogne? We can have dinner there, and you can tell me about yourself.'

'I want to hear about you first,' I said. 'Tell me about your mystery.'

He took a little leather case from his pocket and gave it to me. I opened it. Inside was a photograph of a woman. She was tall and beautiful, with long hair, and large secretive eyes. Her clothes looked very expensive.

'What do you think of that face,' he said. 'Is it an honest face?'

I examined the face in the photograph carefully. It seemed to me to be the face of a woman with a secret. But I could not say if that secret was good or bad. The beauty of the face was full of mystery, and the faint smile on the lips made me think of the smile of the Egyptian Sphinx in the moonlight. Or was it the mysterious smile that you sometimes see on the face of Leonardo's painting, the Mona Lisa, in the Louvre in Paris?

'Well,' he cried impatiently, 'what do you think?'

'A beautiful sphinx,' I answered. 'Tell me all about her.'

'Not now,' he said. 'After dinner.'

When we were drinking our coffee and smoking our cigarettes after dinner, I reminded him, and he told me this story:

'One evening,' he said, 'I was walking down Bond Street in London at about five o'clock. There were a lot of carriages, and the traffic was moving very slowly. There was a small yellow carriage on my side of the road which, for some reason or other, caught my attention. As the carriage passed, I saw the face that I showed you in the photograph earlier. It went straight to my heart. All that night, I thought about the face, and all the next day. I looked for the yellow carriage in the usual places, but I couldn't find it. I began to think that the beautiful stranger was only something from a dream.

'There was a small yellow carriage on my side of the road . . .'

'About a week later, I went to have dinner with Madame de Rastail. Dinner was for eight o'clock, but at half past eight we were still waiting in the sitting room. Finally the servant threw open the door and said "Lady Alroy". A woman entered the room – and it was the woman I was looking for! The woman in the yellow carriage.

'She came into the sitting room very slowly, looking lovely in a grey dress. I was pleased and excited when Madame de Rastail asked me to take Lady Alroy in to dinner. Lady Alroy then sat next to me at the table.

'After we sat down, I said quite innocently, "I think I saw you in Bond Street not long ago, Lady Alroy."

'She became very pale, and said to me in a low voice, "Please don't talk so loudly. Someone may hear you."

'I felt unhappy about such a bad start to our conversation, and I started talking quickly about French theatre and other unimportant things. She spoke very little, always in the same low musical voice. She seemed to be afraid that someone might be listening.

'I fell madly in love, and I was excited by the mystery that seemed to surround her. I wanted to know more – much more – about this mysterious lady.

'She left very soon after dinner, and when she was going, I asked if I could visit her. She said nothing for a moment, looked round to see if anyone was near us, and then said, "Yes. Tomorrow at a quarter to five."

'I asked Madame de Rastail to tell me about her, but I learned only that her husband had died, and she lived in a beautiful house in the most expensive part of London. I left soon after that, and went home.

'The next day I arrived at her London house at exactly a quarter to five. I asked to see Lady Alroy but I was told by a servant that she had just gone out.

'I went to the club, very unhappy and quite confused. After

some thought, I wrote a letter. I asked her if I could try again another afternoon.

'I had no answer for several days, but at last I got a letter saying that I could visit her on Sunday at four o'clock. At the end of the letter there was a strange note: "Please don't write to me here again," it said. "I will explain when I see you."

'On Sunday she was at home when I visited her, and she was perfectly nice to me. But when I was leaving, she said, "If you want to write to me again, will you address your letter to: Mrs Knox, Whitaker's Library, Green Street? There are reasons why I can't receive letters in my own house."

'After that, I saw her often. She continued to be pleasant and mysterious. I thought for a time that she might be in the power of a man, but I could not believe it.

'At last I decided to ask her to be my wife. I wrote to her at the library and asked her to see me the following Monday, at six o'clock. She answered yes, and I was wonderfully happy. I was very much in love with her, you understand. Perhaps because of the mystery surrounding her. No, no, that's not right! I loved the woman. The mystery worried me, it's true. It made me angry.'

'So you discovered the answer to the mystery?' I cried.

'In a way,' he answered. 'On Monday I had lunch with my uncle in his house in Regent's Park. After lunch, I wanted some exercise, and I decided to walk to Piccadilly. The shortest way is through a lot of poor little streets. I was going along one of these when I suddenly saw Lady Alroy in front of me. Her face was half-hidden by a large hat, but there was no doubt in my mind.

'She was walking fast. When she came to the last house in the street, she went up the steps to the front door, took a key from her bag, unlocked the door and went in.

'"So this is the mystery," I said to myself, and I hurried to the front of the house. It seemed to be a place where people can rent rooms.

'She had dropped her handkerchief when she took the key out of her bag. It was lying on the doorstep, and I picked it up and put it in my pocket.

'At six o'clock, I went to see her as we had arranged. She was lying on a sofa in a silver-coloured dress and looked very lovely.

'"I'm so glad to see you," she said. "I haven't been out all day."

'I stared at her, very surprised. I pulled the handkerchief out of my pocket, and gave it to her. "You dropped this in Cumnor Street this afternoon, Lady Alroy," I said very calmly.

'She looked at me in terror, but she didn't take the handkerchief.

'"What were you doing there?" I asked.

'"What right have you to question me?" she answered.

'"The right of a man who loves you," I said. "I came here to ask you to be my wife."

'She hid her face in her hands, but I could see the tears pouring from her eyes.

'"You must tell me," I continued.

'She stood up and, through her tears, she looked straight into my eyes. "Lord Murchison," she said. "There is nothing to tell you."

'"You went to meet somebody!" I cried. "This is your mystery."

'Her face went terribly white, and she said, "I did not go to meet anybody."

'"That's not true," I said.

'"It *is* true," she replied.

'I was mad – completely out of control. I don't know what I said, but I said terrible things to her. Finally I rushed out of the house. She wrote me a letter the next day, but I sent it back unopened, and left for Norway with my friend, Alan Colville.

'After a month in Norway, I returned to London. When I returned I saw in the *Morning Post* newspaper a report about the death of Lady Alroy. She had caught a very bad cold at the theatre one evening, and had died a few days later.

'I shut myself in my rooms and saw nobody for days. I had

'I pulled the handkerchief out of my pocket, and gave it to her.'

loved her so much, so madly. God! I had loved that woman!'

'You went to the street – to the house in it?' I said.

'Yes,' he answered. 'One day I went to Cumnor Street. I had to go. Doubts were destroying my mind. I knocked on the door, and a woman of good appearance opened it. I asked her if she had any rooms to rent.

'"Well, sir," she replied politely, "the sitting room is really taken, but I haven't seen the lady for three months. And the rent hasn't been paid, so I think I can let you have it."

'"Is this the lady?" I asked, and I showed her the photograph.

'"Oh, yes! That's her!" she said. "When is she coming back, sir?"

'"The lady is dead," I replied.

'"Oh dear!" said the woman. "I'm very sorry to hear it. She paid me three pounds a week and she just came and sat in my sitting room sometimes."

'"Did she meet someone here?" I said.

'"No, sir," said the woman. "Never. She always came alone, and she saw nobody."

'"What did she do here?" I cried.

'"She sat in the room, sir, reading books," answered the woman. "Sometimes she had tea, but always alone."

'I didn't know what to say, so I gave the woman five pounds and walked home. What do you think it meant? Do you think the woman's story was true?'

'Yes, I do,' I said.

'Then why did Lady Alroy go there?'

'Gerald,' I answered, 'Lady Alroy was simply a woman who had to have a mystery. She took the room for the pleasure of going there secretly. She imagined that she was a mysterious character in a story. She had a great love of secrets and mysteries, but she herself was just a sphinx without a secret.'

'Do you really think so?' he said.

'I'm sure of it,' I said.

He took the leather case out of his pocket, opened it, and looked at the photograph.

'I'll never be sure,' he said at last.

ACTIVITIES

The Canterville Ghost

Before you read

1 Are there great ghost stories in the literature of your country? Tell your favourite story.

2 Look at the Word List at the back of this book.

    a Which words are useful for the ghost story that you told in Question 1?

    b Find seven words for people.

    c In the past, what did people:

        – travel in?

        – wear to war?

        – fight with?

        – use to light a room?

While you read

3 Write the names of the Otis family's American products beside their purposes.

    a To clean bloodstains from the floor   ....

    b To stop the noise from rusty chains   ....

    c To cure stomach trouble   ....

    d To pour over a ghost and frighten it   ....

4 Who might say these words, an American (A) or a British person (B)?

    a 'It is dangerous to live in a haunted house.'   .....

    b 'Ghosts can make people ill.'   .....

    c 'Money can solve most problems.'   .....

    d 'Ghosts do not exist in our country.'   .....

    e 'We saw a ghost last night. Now we're afraid someone in our family is going to die soon.'   .....

    f 'Please join us for tea in the library.'   .....

    g 'We have a product for every problem.'   .....

    h 'We like our weather. It's always changing.'   .....

    i 'I met a ghost last night and gave him some good advice.'   .....

j 'It's fun to see what the ghost has done each
morning.' .....

k 'Where's my pea-shooter?' .....

l 'I have owned a suit of armour for years and years.' .....

m 'May I introduce myself? I am Sir Robert Jones
and this is my wife, Lady Margaret.' .....

n 'We'd pay a hundred thousand dollars for a family
ghost.' .....

o 'We don't want everything to be new and modern
in our old houses.' .....

After you read

5 Answer these questions about the twins and their methods for
annoying the Canterville ghost.

  a What do they throw at the ghost's head?

  b What do they shoot at him?

  c How do they do with a brush?

  d What do they stretch across passages?

  e What do they put on the top of the stairs?

  f What do they put on the top of their bedroom door?

  g What do they scream at the ghost?

6 Who says these words? Who or what are they talking about?

  a 'It's been famous for three centuries – since 1584.'

  b 'Pinkerton's Wonder Stain Cleaner will clean it in a second.'

  c 'Well, I'll make them sorry! Oh, yes, I will!'

  d 'If you behave yourself, no-one will annoy you.'

  e '...she was a bad housekeeper. She knew nothing about
cooking.'

  f 'There the grass grows long and deep, and there are the white
stars of wild flowers.'

  g 'My dear little girl, thank God you're safe.'

  h 'God has forgiven him.'

  i 'I must ask you to take them to London with you. Virginia asks
for only one thing – the box in which they were kept.'

  j 'You can have your secret if I can have your heart.'

7 How did the ghost frighten these people in the past?

    a Lord Canterville's aunt

    b four girl servants

    c a man-servant

    d Lady Stutfield

    e Lord Raker and three servants

    f Lady Barbara Modish

    g Old Lady Startup

8 How does the ghost plan to frighten the Otis family on Friday, 17th August?

    a Washington

    b Mrs Otis

    c Mr Otis

    d Virginia

    e the twins

9 What do you know about the marriages between these people? Which couple do you think is the happiest?

    a Hiram and Lucretia Otis

    b Sir Simon and Lady Eleanore de Canterville

    c Cecil and Virginia, the Duke and Duchess of Cheshire

10 Work with another student and act out this conversation. One of you is the ghost of Sir Simon de Canterville and the other is Virginia Otis. You are in the little room where Virginia finds the ghost and you talk about death. Then you go into the great black hole that appears when the wall slowly opens. What do you talk about there? How does Virginia return to her family?

Lord Arthur Savile's Crime

Before you read

11 A chiromantist tells fortunes by reading people's hands. What other methods do fortune tellers use? Have you ever had your fortune told? Do you believe in fortune-telling?

12 Part of the title of this story is *A Study of Duty*. What duties do most people feel responsible for? Do you believe you have a duty to obey society's rules and laws or to obey certain people?

While you read

13 Who is it? Read the description and write the correct name.

 a Forty years old; enjoys pleasure;
  famous hostess   ....

 b Young, tall, handsome; not
  especially clever, but very romantic ....

 c Unattractive little chiromantist; has
  green eyes and wears gold glasses ....

 d Lady Windermere's friend; fat
  hand with short square fingers;
  strong sense of duty   ....

 e Cheerful, adventurous; has a
  second wife; hates cats   ....

 f Beautiful girl; sweet, innocent with
  dreamy eyes; in love   ....

 g Reads French story-books; has
  stomach trouble; hates doctors
  but loves medicines   ....

 h Lord Arthur Savile's brother;
  travels in Italy   ....

 i Important churchman; has a
  clock collection   ....

 j Rough-looking German; makes
  bombs; lives for art, not money ....

After you read

14 Follow Lord Arthur Savile from the beginning of the story until Lady
 Clementine's death. In which order does he visit these places?

 a Pestle and Humbey's

 b Venice-Ravenna-Venice

 c Lady Windermere's party

 d His club

 e Sybil Merton's house

 f His house in Belgrave Square

 g Lady Clementina's house

15 Match Lord Savile's activities with the places in Question 14.

    a He is waiting for news of Lady Clementina's death.

    b He buys a capsule of aconitine.

    c He intends to poison the old lady.

    d He delays his wedding to the young lady.

    e He studies Erskine's book on poisons.

    f He hears some frightening news from Mr Podgers.

    g He decides who he will murder.

16 Why are these important when Lord Savile tries to murder his uncle, the Dean of Chichester?

    a The dean's collection of clocks

    b Rouvaloff

    c A small golden figure of Liberty

    d Five pounds

    e Jane Percy

17 What:

    a frightens a number of people at Lady Windermere's party?

    b does the chiromantist see in Lord Arthur's hands?

    c is aconitine?

    d does Lord Arthur do in Venice?

    e does Lord Arthur use to try to kill his uncle?

    f happens to Mr Podgers?

    g does Lady Windermere think of chiromancy at the end of the story?

18 Discuss these questions.

    a Read these statements by Lady Windermere. What do they tell us about her character?

    'Nothing interesting is ever quite right.'

    'All my guests do what I tell them to do.'

    'A future wife ought not to know everything about the man she's going to marry.'

    'Nobody cares about relatives who aren't close these days – it's not fashionable.'

    'I've never heard anything so silly in all my life.'

b What do these sentences tell us about Lord Arthur's character?

He was glad that he had done the right thing.

Next, he would have to try a bomb. That seemed sensible.

Lord Arthur hated pretending.

'I've tried to do my duty!'

'Because of chiromancy, I have all the happiness in my life.'

19 Work with another student. Act out this conversation.

Student A: You are Lord Arthur Savile. You are happy because you have thrown Mr Podgers over the bridge. Tell your brother about the murder.

Student B: You are Lord Surbiton, Lord Arthur Savile's brother. You are shocked by your brother's news. Ask him about his reasons for murdering Mr Podgers.

The Sphinx Without a Secret

Before you read

20 What does a sphinx look like? Where can you find one? How is a sphinx connected to secrets and mysteries?

21 List the most important things for a good relationship with a husband/wife or close friend. How high on the list would you put trust? How can secrets and lies cause problems in a relationship?

While you read

22 Circle the correct answer.

a The storyteller and Lord Murchison become friends in *Oxford/Paris*.

b Lord Murchison prefers to travel in a *yellow/green* carriage.

c Lady Alroy's smile makes the storyteller think of *two/three* famous works of art.

d Lord Murchison sees Lady Alroy for the first time when she is *at a party/in a carriage*.

e Madame de Rastail tells Lord Murchison that Lady Alroy is *unmarried and rich/married and poor*.

f On the day after Madame de Rastail's party, Lord Murchison *meets/doesn't meet* Lady Alroy at her London house.

g After several visits to Lady Alroy's London house, Lord Murchison decides to *ask her to marry him / stop seeing her.*

h Lady Alroy drops *her key / her handkerchief* on Cumnor Street.

i Lord Murchison writes *many / no* letters to Lady Alroy after she lies to him about Cumnor Street.

j Lord Murchison is in *Norway / London* when he learns about Lady Alroy's death.

k Before her death, Lady Alroy pays *three / five* pounds a week to rent the sitting room in Cumnor Street.

l The storyteller thinks that Lady Alroy rents a room in Cumnor Street because she *pretends to have / has many dark* secrets.

After you read

23 Discuss these questions.

a Why does Lord Murchison fall in love with Lady Alroy? Make a list of reasons.

b In your opinion, does Lord Murchison have enough good reasons for wanting to marry Lady Alroy?

c Do you believe in love at first sight? Why (not)?

24 Discuss how you think Lord Murchison feels in each of these situations.

a On an afternoon outside the Café de la Paix in Paris when he meets his old friend from Oxford University

b Walking down Bond Street in London when he sees Lady Alroy in a yellow carriage

c At a dinner party at Madame de Rastail's house when he meets Lady Alroy

d At Lady Alroy's house for the first time when he learns that she is not at home

e After several visits to Lady Alroy's house when he decides he wants to marry her

f On his walk to Piccadilly to meet Lady Alroy when he sees her on a poor little street

g At Lady Alroy's house when she lies to him about her visit to Cumnor Street

h When he reads about the death of Lady Alroy

i At the house on Cumnor Street after Lady Alroy's death when he learns about her secret

25 Discuss these questions.

   a No one in this story uses the title *Mr* or *Mrs* (Mrs Knox at Whitaker's Library is not a real person.) What three titles are used?

   b Think about the titles that people use in 'The Canterville Ghost' and in 'Lord Arthur Savile's Crime'. What do these titles tell us about Oscar Wilde and his short stories?

Writing

26 You are Virginia Otis and you have lived at Canterville Chase for two weeks. Write a letter to a school friend in the United States. Tell her about the house, the bloodstain in the library and your missing paints. Tell her what you think is happening. Also tell her about the young Duke of Cheshire.

27 You are Mrs Umney and the Otis family are the first Americans you have ever met. Write to your sister and tell her about some of their strange, foreign beliefs and habits.

28 Write the ghost story that you told in Activity 1. Use words from the Word List at the back of this book.

29 You are a film-writer and you want to write a film with ghosts in it. Make a list of horrible ways for your ghosts to frighten people. Describe what the ghosts will look like.

30 You witnessed Lord Arthur Savile throwing a man into the River Thames. Write a statement for the police. Give descriptions of the men if you can.

31 Write about Lady Windermere's and Lord Arthur Savile's different opinions on chiromancy at the end of their story. Include your own opinion on the subject and explain your reasons.

32 You are Lady Alroy. Lord Murchison discovers your secret visits to a house on Cumnor Street. He becomes very angry and says some terrible things. Decide what you think of him. Do you want to marry him or not? Write a letter to him after he rushes out of your house.

33 You are Lord Murchison and you are now married to a sensible woman who you love very much. She finds your photograph of Lady Alroy. Explain your reasons for keeping the photograph in the special little leather case in your pocket.

34 The first two stories have happy endings. Write a happy ending for 'The Sphinx Without a Secret'.

35 Describe how Oscar Wilde writes about death in these three stories. How is this subject both important and amusing?

WORD LIST

aconitine (n) one of the strongest poisons that come from plants

alarm clock (n) a clock that makes a noise to wake you up

ambassador (n) an important official that a government sends to another country to manage its relationship with that country

armour (n) metal protective clothing worn during fighting in the past

burial sheet (n) a sheet that is put around a dead body before the body is placed in the ground

candle (n) a white or coloured stick that you burn to produce light

capsule (n) a small, rounded container

carriage (n) a vehicle pulled by one or more horses

chain (n/v) metal rings connected in a line

chiromancy (n) the art of telling the future by looking at a person's hand; a **chiromantist** is the person who does this

dean (n) a man with a high position in the Church of England; his job is to manage a large church

duchess (n) a woman with the highest social position below a princess, or the wife of a duke

duke (n) a man with the highest social position below a prince

explode (v) to break into pieces violently and with a loud noise, causing damage

haunt (v) (of ghosts) to appear somewhere regularly

lawyer (n) a professional who gives advice about the law and speaks for people in court

liberty (n) the state of being free to live your life as you want to

passage (n) a long, narrow area that connects two or more rooms

pray (v) to speak to God, to ask for help or thank Him

rise (v) to go up

rub (v) to move across something while pressing against it

rusty (adj) covered with something red or brown that forms on wet metal

scar (n) a mark on your skin from an old cut

skeleton (n) all the connected bones in a human or animal body

sphinx (n) an old Egyptian figure of an animal with a human head

stain (n) a mark that is difficult to clean away

sword (n) a long, sharp knife that was used for fighting in the past

trust (v) to believe that someone will not lie to you or hurt you

twins (n pl) two children who are born at the same time to the same mother

will (n) the legal document that says who will receive your property after your death